J.P. and the STINKY MONSTER

ANA CRESPO

Pictures by
ERICA SIROTICH

Albert Whitman & Company
Chicago, Illinois

Other books in the MY EMOTIONS and ME series:

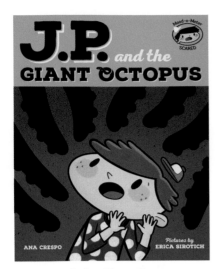

JP and the Giant Octopus:
Feeling Afraid

JP and the Polka-Dotted Aliens:
Feeling Angry

JP and the Bossy Dinosaur:
Feeling Sad

To the two stinky monsters of my life–Dudu and Titi—AC

For Oma and Opa—ES

Library of Congress Cataloging-in-Publication
data is on file with the publisher.

Text copyright © 2016 by Ana Crespo
Pictures copyright © 2016 by Albert Whitman & Company
Pictures by Erica Sirotich
Published in 2016 by Albert Whitman & Company
ISBN 978-0-8075-3979-8

Printed in China
10 9 8 7 6 5 4 3 2 1 HH 25 24 23 22 21 20 19 18 17 16

Design by Jordan Kost

For more information about Albert Whitman & Company,
visit our web site at www.albertwhitman.com

I am JP the dog.

I am nice. I am helpful.

I am loving.

But sometimes I forget I am a loving dog.
Sometimes I feel jealous.

Like when a monster
tried to keep my grandma
away from me.

The monster was all slimy and wiggly.

It made weird noises.

It was super stinky.

And it wouldn't leave my grandma alone.

I was so jealous!

The stinky monster was
ruining my day.
I wanted to go back home.

Then I remembered I am a loving dog.

I made some doggie faces.

I sang some doggie songs.

I played some doggie games.

The stinky monster smiled.

I even got to hold it.

And it fell asleep.

Grandma and I had a few minutes to ourselves.

We enjoyed every single one of them.

I am JP.

I am nice. I am helpful.

Sometimes I feel jealous…

but I know I am loved.

A Note to Parents and Teachers from the Author

Jealousy is a common and normal feeling usually associated with competition. In JP's case, he is competing with his new baby cousin for Grandma's attention. However, no matter how normal it is, jealousy can bring forward some bad feelings, such as anger or rejection, and learning to deal with it can be helpful.

Here are some ways to help your child work through jealousy:

Acknowledge your child's feelings. This is an important step to help your child recognize his emotions. It is likely that the child will not understand what he is feeling or why. Share examples that show how jealousy is a common emotion. You can do this by sharing your own memories or reading stories such as JP's. **Ask questions.** When you read a story or share a memory, questions can help children understand their own feelings. *Why is JP jealous? What would you do if you were JP?*

Show her she is loved. A child who is introduced to a new addition to the family, for example, may feel rejected. Although the change brings a new routine to the household, try to maintain certain rituals that will assure the child that she is still loved. If you enjoy baking together like JP and his grandma, do it more often. If you read a book every night, continue that tradition.

However, jealousy is not always due to a change in the family. Sometimes kids will feel jealous of a friend who is a faster runner or a better artist. **Praise your child's accomplishments.** If she doesn't win the race, for instance, show how she improved her own time. **Nurture her strengths.** Maybe her drawing is not great, but her color choices are beautiful or her storytelling is spot on. Focus on the positives and encourage her to keep practicing. Also encourage her to try additional ways to express her creativity—singing, dancing, theater, etc. Practicing will help your child improve her skills. Experimenting will help your child find her strengths. Both will give her confidence.

The goal is to help your child understand that people's needs, goals, and talents are different. There will be times when one sibling will need more attention than the other. There will be those who aim to win and those who aim to improve themselves. There will always be those talented with a pencil and those talented with numbers.

Of course, this is a difficult concept to understand. But you can help your child make the best of the situation. A child who knows how to deal with jealousy will eventually seek attention through positive behavior, share more easily, be more caring, and learn self-acceptance.

Please note that I am not a specialist in the field of children's emotions. My experience and knowledge come from being a parent and conducting my own research. For additional information specific to your needs, please seek a professional opinion.

References:

Child Youth Health. "Jealousy." July 2014. http://www.cyh.com/HealthTopics/HealthTopicDetailsKids.aspx?p=335&np=287&id=2599

Dr. Michele Borba. "Seven Ways to Reduce Sibling Jealousy." Dr. Michele Borba. 2002. http://micheleborba.com/Pages/ArtBMI18.htm

PBS Kids. "Sibling Rivalry: The Jealousy Monster." It's My Life. 2005. http://pbskids.org/itsmylife/family/sibrivalry/article3.html